IT WAS LIKE A BAD DREAM
OR A GOOD HORROR MOVIE.

The slime started seeping out of the TV set.

Arnold wanted to wake up or change the channel, but he couldn't take his eyes off the slimy stuff. It seemed to be taking on a human form. Arnold hoped he was just imagining it.

Then the slimy human form started to grow and turn solid. Arnold definitely wasn't imagining it.

His eyes opened wide. He turned and ran.

Too late! The human form grabbed him by the wrist and would not let go.

"Hey!" boomed a voice that actually sounded human. "Don't change that channel!"

It's New!
It's Improved!
It's Terrible!

Stephen Manes

A BANTAM SKYLARK BOOK®
NEW YORK • TORONTO • LONDON • SYDNEY • AUCKLAND

RL 4, 007–011

IT'S NEW! IT'S IMPROVED! IT'S TERRIBLE!

A Bantam Skylark Book / April 1989

*Skylark Books is a registered trademark of Bantam Books,
a division of Bantam Doubleday Dell Publishing Group, Inc.
Registered in U.S. Patent and Trademark Office and elsewhere.*

ISBN 0-553-15682-9

Published simultaneously in the United States and Canada

Bantam Books are published by Bantam Books, a division of Bantam Doubleday
Dell Publishing Group, Inc. Its trademark, consisting of the words "Bantam
Books" and the portrayal of a rooster, is Registered in U.S. Patent and Trade-
mark Office and in other countries. Marca Registrada. Bantam Books, 666 Fifth
Avenue, New York, New York 10103.

PRINTED IN THE UNITED STATES OF AMERICA

CW   14 13 12 11 10 9 8 7 6 5 4

for Judy

It's New!
It's Improved!
It's Terrible!

1

They were *new*! They were *improved*! They were *amazing*! They were neat. Arnold Schlemp had to have them. That was all there was to it. If he didn't get them, he would die. Or worse.

Arnold moved up to the TV for a closer look. There was no doubt about it. Helicopter Shoes were the greatest footwear in the universe.

The yellow helicopters on the high tops actually glowed in the dark. The zigzag designs on the shoelaces even glowed in the daytime. The soles had a secret bounce-gas that made you jump as high as humanly possible. And they were very, very expensive—which meant they just had to be great! They were the exact same basketball shoes Ralph "Helicopter" Jones wore, except his were size 17.

In the commercials Helicopter Jones sang

1

and danced and boogied and shot hoops with a bunch of kids Arnold's age. The kids looked happier than anyone Arnold had ever met. The reason had to be their Helicopter Shoes.

When you put them on your feet, magic happened. If you didn't wear them, you couldn't be cool. Helicopter Jones said so himself. They were New! IMPROVED! *Amazing! NEAT!*

Arnold had to have them. He just had to. That was all there was to it. Period. Exclamation point.

Boy, did he ever want those shoes!

2

"**F**orget it!" said Arnold's father. "Don't even think about it! For that kind of money you can buy six pairs of regular basketball shoes."

"And two basketballs to go with them," added Arnold's mother.

"Not shoes like these," Arnold insisted. "These are the greatest shoes in the galaxy."

His father scowled. "If you develop the greatest feet in the galaxy, perhaps we'll consider it."

"Lots of kids have these shoes," Arnold declared. Actually the only kids he had ever seen wearing those shoes were the ones in the commercials.

"Rich kids maybe." His father snorted. "Rich we are not."

Arnold sighed. "Helicopter Jones wears these shoes."

"Helicopter Jones gets paid to wear them," Arnold's father pointed out. "And he makes seventeen zillion dollars a year just for playing a game."

Arnold's mother chimed in. "With that kind of money, he could afford those shoes even if he didn't get paid to wear them."

Arnold's father chuckled. "He might even be able to afford *two* pairs."

Arnold didn't think it was funny at all. He was stuck plodding around in his plain old ordinary sneakers. They didn't glow in the daytime. They didn't even glow in the dark. They didn't have yellow helicopters or special bounce-gas soles. They didn't make magic happen. Worst of all, they didn't wear out.

But neither did Arnold. Every time he went to the mall, he marched straight to the Shoeperman Shoppe and stared at the display window. The shoes looked even more magical in person than they did on TV. He had to try them on. He had to. But the store wouldn't even let him touch something that expensive without his parents, and his parents weren't interested.

"Just for one minute?" he begged.

"Forget it," said his mother.

"Please? Just for ten seconds? Just so I can try out the bounce-gas?"

"Arnold, you are giving *me* bounce-gas," said his father. "No, and that's final."

But it wasn't final. Not as far as Arnold was concerned. Not by a jump shot.

3

Arnold's birthday was only three weeks away. "You're in luck," declared his best friend, Eddie Magistretti. "I know a foolproof plan. It works every time."

"I sure hope you're right," said Arnold.

"I'm telling you, it works great," Eddie insisted. "I got my camera, didn't I?"

"You can get five cameras like that for the price of one pair of Helicopter Shoes," Arnold pointed out.

"They're *that* expensive?" Eddie scoffed. "They can't be worth it!"

Arnold told him all about the zigzag shoelaces and the yellow helicopters and the bounce-gas soles and Helicopter Jones. Eddie just shrugged. "Shoes are shoes."

"You have to see them in person," Arnold claimed. "You have to try them on."

Eddie shrugged. "All right. I almost believe you. Anyhow, here's what to do."

Arnold followed Eddie's instructions exactly. "GREAT BIRTHDAY PRESENTS ACCORDING TO ARNOLD SCHLEMP" he typed at the top of the screen on the computer at school. Then he banged out a list:

WaterMusic
UgliBoard
HELICOPTER SHOES!!!!!

He printed the list five times on the computer printer. Then every day for five days he accidentally on purpose dropped one copy where his parents would be sure to find it.

And just to make sure they got the most important part of the message, Arnold walked around humming the Helicopter Shoes song. His parents pretended to ignore him, but he was sure they were only fooling. He was absolutely positive that in just a few days he'd be jumping around on bounce-gas soles.

On birthday morning his mom and dad woke him up by singing "Happy Birthday to You!" Around him on the bed were gift-wrapped boxes—three of them. Perfect! His hints must have worked!

The first present Arnold opened didn't have anything to do with shoes. It was WaterMusic—the radio and tape player that can play underwater and comes complete with a built-in squirt gun. It was the first thing on Arnold's list. So far, so good.

The second present was an UgliBoard—the skateboard with disgusting knobby wart-wheels and repulsive monster faces you can change in less than fifteen seconds. It was the second item on Arnold's list. So far, even better.

Arnold knew the big third package could only be one thing. He tore at the ribbons. He was positive that any second he'd be seeing yellow helicopters and glowing zigzag shoelaces. His heart thumped as he tossed the wrapping paper aside and tore open the lid.

But the only thing in the box was a brand-new basketball. It was a great basketball—the best one he'd ever seen. It even had Helicopter Jones's autograph on it. But it wasn't a pair of Helicopter Shoes. Not even close, really.

How could his parents do this to him? Arnold felt awful. He felt cheated. He felt gypped.

But he tried not to show it. He thanked his parents for the presents. They smiled and wished him happy birthday again. Then they told him to be sure to hurry down to breakfast.

Breakfast? Of course! Now he knew what

8

was going on—they were saving the Helicopter Shoes for a surprise. The shoelaces were probably already glowing at the breakfast table! Arnold put on his bathrobe and ran downstairs.

Something special was waiting for him in the dining room, all right: his favorite breakfast of sausage and home-fried potatoes and taco sauce with waffles and ice cream. But there weren't any Helicopter Shoes to be seen. Not even one shoe. Not even a shoelace.

Arnold's breakfast tasted kind of bitter. As he was forcing it down, he heard a shout of "Happy birthday, Arnold!" from the front door. Eddie came inside and handed Arnold a small gift-wrapped package.

"Thanks," Arnold said glumly.

Eddie looked down at Arnold's feet. "Wait a minute!" he said. "It didn't work?"

Arnold sighed. "Not the important part."

"Unbelievable!" Eddie made a face. "Maybe you'd better not open that package."

But Arnold had already opened it. Inside was a spray can of special basketball-shoe cleaner and preservative. "I thought it would be the perfect thing," Eddie said.

Arnold shrugged. "It would have been great. If the rest of the plan had worked. Thanks."

It just wasn't fair, Arnold kept thinking as he

and Eddie took turns squirting each other with his WaterMusic and riding his UgliBoard and throwing baskets with his new ball. They were all great presents, no doubt about it. But every time he glanced down at his feet, Arnold felt like crying.

4

Birthday dinner that evening was turkey—
Arnold's second-favorite food. But it tasted
kind of stale somehow. Birthday dessert was his
number one favorite: quadruple-chocolate
mousse cake with quintuple-chocolate icing. But
it didn't look as chocolaty or as special as it usu-
ally did.

Arnold sighed and made a desperate wish.
He blew out all the candles. But he was positive
his wish wouldn't come true.

Then his mother put a gift-wrapped box on
the table. "It came in the mail this afternoon. It's
from Grandma."

Arnold didn't even want to open it. There
had to be a jacket inside. Grandma always gave
him jackets. They were okay jackets, and sometimes even better than okay, like last year's Car-

dinals baseball warm-up. But they weren't Helicopter Shoes.

Arnold sighed and tore at the wrapping. What was inside didn't smell like clothes. In fact, it smelled kind of rubbery. Kind of like . . . (Arnold was sure he was imagining it) . . . a pair of . . . it couldn't be! It was!

Helicopter Shoes! WOW!

Arnold's candle-blowing wish had come true. The shoes fit perfectly. The zigzag shoelaces blazed in the light. The shoes looked ten times better than they did on TV or even in the shop window.

Arnold sang the Helicopter Shoes song and pranced around the living room. The bounce-gas soles made him feel as though he were dancing on air. He bounced down to the basement. He turned out all the lights. The helicopters glowed in the dark. They really did. Neat!

"These shoes are really fantastic!" Arnold shouted as he bounced back up the stairs.

"We'll call Grandma later on," said his mother. "You can tell her what you think of them."

"You bet!" Arnold exclaimed. "I'll thank her a million times! This is the best birthday ever!"

Arnold felt terrific! He went upstairs and got his new basketball from the closet. He bounced outside. He hummed the Helicopter Shoes song every step of the way to Eddie's house.

"It worked!" he shouted. "I don't know how, but it worked!"

"Told you," said Eddie, looking at Arnold's feet. "They do look kind of neat, all right."

"They're super!" Arnold said. "Let's go down to the playground."

Eddie brought his camera and took pictures. Arnold dribbled like a pro. He shot like a wizard. He was cool. He was the next Helicopter Jones. Hey, he *was* Helicopter Jones! He could make any shot he wanted to. Five in a row! Six in a row! Seven—well, even the original Helicopter Jones missed once in a while.

"You want to try them on?" Arnold asked.

"Are you kidding? Remember when Coach started joking about my enormous shoes? I may be shorter than you, but my feet are three sizes bigger."

Arnold frowned. "I forgot."

"It's okay," Eddie said. "I don't get real excited about shoes even if they do glow in the daytime."

The daytime was fading. Arnold "Helicopter" Schlemp said good-bye to Eddie and boogied toward home. But as he crossed the street, the sole of his left foot felt kind of funny.

There had to be a stone or something in his shoe.

Arnold sat down on the curb, took the shoe off, held it upside down, and shook it hard. Nothing fell out. He put his hand inside and felt around, but he didn't find anything there. When he put the shoe on again, the stone or whatever it was seemed to have gone away.

But when he got home, his foot felt funny again. Arnold took his shoe off and then his sock. Right in the middle of the sole of his left foot was a huge red bubble of a blister.

Then his other foot began to hurt. He took a look. An even bigger blister was popping out of his right heel. He rubbed it a little. It burned. But he knew it couldn't be the shoes' fault. He probably needed Helicopter Socks or something.

He put his left sock and shoe back on. His foot didn't feel too bad, as long as he didn't step down too hard. He turned on the TV. Kids began dancing and singing in his very favorite commercial:

Helicopter
Helicopter
Helicopter Shoes.

We're talking
Helicopter
Helicopter
Helicopter Shoes.

Arnold eased his foot back into his other shoe so he could sing and bounce-gas along. Helicopter Jones came right up to the screen:

Hey, Helicopter here
And I just want to say
My Helicopter Shoes
Are the shoes of today!

You can dance and jump around
In any old shoes.
But mine are the ones
That will cure your blues.

Arnold tapped his foot to the music. His sole started burning again. The gang of happy kids came forward on the screen.

Helicopter
Helicopter
Helicopter Shoes.

We're talking
Helicopter
Helicopter
Helicopter Shoes.

Arnold adjusted his zigzag shoelaces, but his right shoe still felt funny. He gave the tongue a gentle tug. It ripped right off the shoe. Heli-

15

copter Jones came front and center again on the screen.

My shoes are the best
And that's the truth.
You gotta move with the 'Copter
Or else you're uncouth.

Without these shoes
I couldn't be great
They're the shoes
That let me levitate.

The entire tongue of his brand-new shoe just dangled there in Arnold's fingers. It was terrible. Arnold couldn't believe it. On the screen, Helicopter Jones went up for a shot.

Hey, I made the shot
And so will you
As long as you're wearing
My Helicopter shoe.

Arnold just stared at his ruined shoe and its broken tongue. The kids on TV danced up front and laughed. It was as though they were laughing at Arnold and his faulty footwear.

Helicopter

Helicopter
Helicopter Shoes.

Arnold was furious. He threw the tongue toward them. It fluttered to the floor in front of the TV set. The tongue seemed to be sticking out at him, making fun of him.

We're talking
Helicopter
Helicopter
Helicopter Shoes.

"Shut up!" Arnold screamed. He took off his tongueless shoe and flung it toward the screen.

Heli . . . CRASH!

A perfect hit! First Arnold heard a loud "Pop!" Next he heard the tinkle of glass. Then the screen exploded inward.

"Uh-oh," said Arnold Schlemp.

"Are you all right?" his mother shouted from upstairs. "We heard a noise."

"I'm okay," Arnold shouted back. "Honest!" A hazy golden light began to shimmer in the broken TV set.

"How are the famous shoes?" his mother hollered.

"Fine!" Arnold lied as the light in the broken TV set grew brighter.

"Maybe we should call Grandma to thank her!" his mother shouted.

"I'll come upstairs in a couple of minutes," Arnold shouted back. "There's something I want to finish watching first!"

The last thing Arnold wanted was his parents' checking out the living room. It wasn't just the broken TV set. It was also the strange golden light inside it. The light was turning solid and kind of slimy—sort of like golden ginger-ale Jell-O. Then the slime started seeping out of the TV set.

It was like a bad dream or a good horror movie. Arnold wanted to wake up or change the channel, but he couldn't take his eyes off the slimy stuff. It seemed to be taking on a human form. Arnold hoped he was just imagining it.

Then the slimy human form started to grow and turn solid. Arnold definitely wasn't imagining it.

His eyes opened wide. He turned and ran.

Too late! The human form grabbed him by the wrist and would not let go.

18

5

"Hey!" boomed a voice that actually sounded human. "Don't change that channel!"

Arnold was almost afraid to look, but he forced himself to turn around. Somehow all the slime was gone. The voice belonged to a boy his own age. The boy was tall and skinny and blond. He had bright blue eyes and a big smile on his face. He was wearing a Helicopter Jones T-shirt and a pair of Helicopter Jones jeans and—of course—Helicopter Shoes!

The mysterious stranger let go of Arnold's wrist, whirled smoothly, and broke into song:

Helicopter
Helicopter
Helicopter Shoes

We're talking
Helicopter
Helicopter
Helicopter Shoes.

He spun around gracefully, stopped short, and flashed his big smile at Arnold.

"You're from the commercial!" Arnold exclaimed.

"Not just one commercial!" said the stranger, smiling even wider. "Not just two commercials! Not merely three! Hey, I'm in twenty different commercials, each one more wonderful than the next! Isn't that amazing?"

Arnold was too flabbergasted to say anything.

The stranger extended his hand. "You're my special friend."

Arnold suddenly remembered: This kid had said those exact same words in last year's commercials for those ugly prune-faced dolls. "I don't even know you," Arnold replied suspiciously. "How'd you get here? Where'd you come from?"

The smiling stranger did a silent tap on the carpet. He whirled around and sang:

I come from here
I come from there

But I can come
From anywhere.

"Costumes sold separately," he added confidentially in a deeper voice.

Arnold recognized that, too. It was the commercial for Mr. Mysterio, the amazing spy action-figure. "Who are you?" Arnold demanded.

The stranger bowed deeply. "Will Flack, at your service," he said through his dazzling smile. "Now, just tell me one thing. What exactly are we selling?"

"Selling? I'm not selling anything," said Arnold. "Unless maybe you're interested in a broken pair of Helicopter Shoes."

"Broken? What?"

Arnold picked up his tongueless Helicopter shoe and handed it to Will. "Broken. Messed-up. Ruined."

Will's eyes brightened. "Of course! This is our never-before-offered detachable-tongue model. It's new! It's improved! It's—"

"Terrible!" Arnold interrupted.

"Terrible?"

"Terrible," Arnold repeated.

"Terrible? That's not terrible!" Will boomed cheerfully. "Terrible is Worgo, The Terrible Monstrosaur. He crushes! *KRRRRRASH!*" He crumbles! *KRRRRRRACK!* He chomps! *MMMM-*

21

MMMUNCH. He's new from ToySel! (Batteries sold separately)."

"Shhh," said Arnold, "not so loud."

"He's so amazing, I want to shout it from the rooftops!" Will hollered again.

"Arnold, we've told you a thousand times!" shouted Mr. Schlemp from upstairs. "Turn down that TV set!"

TV set? What a laugh! Arnold took another look at it. The TV set was a shambles. It lay on the floor in a heap of broken glass. How could he ever explain it? Or this kid who had magically appeared in a cloud of slime? The very last thing Arnold needed was for his parents to come downstairs right now.

"Shhh!" he whispered to Will.

"Arnold, did you hear me?" Mr. Schlemp shouted.

"Sorry!" Arnold hollered back. "I turned it down already."

"Thank you!" his father shouted sarcastically. Arnold heard him slam the bedroom door.

"Grouchy? Now there's a cure for your blues!" Will said cheerily. "Just—"

"Would you stop imitating commercials for one second?" Arnold interrupted. "I want to know how you got here."

22

"Don't be silly. You know why I'm here. I'm going to be in your commercial."

"My commercial? What commercial?"

"Stop kidding. You know what commercial. Any minute now we'll jump right into action. Now, what am I supposed to do? What are we selling?"

"We're not selling anything," Arnold said. "I live here."

"Sure you do. At least while this commercial's on." Will looked around. "I know! TV sets! That broken one over there will magically turn brand-new."

Arnold shuddered. "I wish."

"No problem!" Will beamed. "All I need is the script. Or I can just make something up. Let's see . . . 'It's magic! Make your old TV set just like new with . . .' What are we selling again?"

"I told you. We're not selling anything."

"Right! A public service announcement! 'Lend a hand! Donate your used TV to the charity of your choice! Just phone the number on your screen.'"

"There *is* no number," Arnold insisted. "There *is* no screen."

"You can't fool me," said Will. "I eat Brain Berries, the cereal that gives you the smarts."

"I keep telling you," Arnold replied exasperatedly. "This isn't a commercial. My TV just broke. And somehow you came through it from the inside."

Will kept smiling. "Wait a minute! Your T-shirt! It doesn't say anything on it."

"So what?"

"It has to say something on it. Or at least have some little character on the front. It has to. It's a sacred rule."

"Maybe in commercials," Arnold said. "But I keep telling you: This isn't a commercial. This is real life."

"I don't know what you're talking about," Will insisted. "But whatever it is, it's easy to fix. You need . . . now just let me think . . ."

Arnold knew exactly what he needed. He needed somebody to come and fix the TV set in about ten seconds. And somebody to tell him what he was supposed to do with this weird kid.

Arnold needed fast, FAST, *FAST RELIEF.* But he didn't expect to get it.

6

"**A**rnold!" hollered his mother from upstairs. "Your father asked you to turn
down the TV. And while we're on the subject,
maybe you could stop talking back to it?"

"Okay!" Arnold shouted. But he could hear
his mother heading toward the top of the stairs.

Arnold grabbed Will's arm. "Stand right
here," he said. "Whatever you do, stay right beside me. Don't move. If we don't stand here and
hide that broken TV set from my mom, you're
really going to find out how awful things can
be."

"I'm cool," Will said calmly. "I'm hip."

"And are you ready to phone Grand . . ."
Halfway down the stairs, Arnold's mom saw Will
and stopped short. "Who's this?"

"Will Flack, at your service." He started to
bow, but Arnold nudged him in the ribs. "De-

lighted to meet you," Will added sweetly. "I'm sure we'll get along smashingly!"

"I'm sure we will," said Mrs. Schlemp with a sigh. "But Arnold, it's almost bedtime. What's this friend of yours doing here at this hour?"

"He just sort of dropped in," Arnold said nervously.

Mr. Schlemp came halfway downstairs, too. "Aha! I see your friend is wearing a certain well-known shoe. Is this some sort of club?"

"Right," Arnold lied. "People with these shoes sort of hang out together."

Will sang:

It's no use booing
And no use hissing
Without Helicopter Shoes
You don't know what you're missing.

Arnold was positive Will would whirl or spin around and spoil everything. But he didn't.

"You sound amazingly like a certain com-mercial," said Mr. Schlemp.

"Thank you," said Will, beaming.

"One we have heard perhaps a bit too often around this household," said Mr. Schlemp, star-ing directly at Arnold.

Arnold didn't say a word.

26

"Do Will's parents know he's here?" Mrs. Schlemp inquired.

"Sure," Arnold lied. "We phoned them a little while ago."

"With our new evening rates, it's the same great service at an even better low price!" Will pointed out proudly.

Arnold's mother scowled. "And his parents said it's okay if he sleeps over on a school night?"

"Okay? More than okay! It's um-diddle-super!" chirped the surprise guest.

Mr. Schlemp scowled. "I can almost believe that."

Arnold glared at Will. "They said okay," he lied.

Arnold's mother sighed. "Well, I suppose it's okay with us then. Get the sleeping bag out of the basement. But remember, no staying up late. Birthday or no birthday, you still have to get up bright and early for school."

"Bright and early!" said Will. "That's when Golden O.J. shines!"

"Does this friend of yours have a remote-control off switch?" asked Mr. Schlemp. Arnold frowned.

"Don't forget to turn out the downstairs lights," said Mrs. Schlemp. "Your father and I are going to bed. Good night."

"You'll have the sleep of your life and wake up feeling refreshed," Will assured them.

"I certainly hope so." Arnold's father shook his head as he went up the stairs.

What a birthday! Arnold thought. *First the greatest present ever gives me two awful blisters and falls apart. Then the TV set breaks. Then the weirdest kid on the planet comes through the hole in the TV. Why me?*

"You're my special friend," Will repeated with all the sincerity of a TV commercial. Arnold dragged his "special friend" into the kitchen before he could cause any more trouble.

7

Arnold poured two glasses of milk and uncovered the cake. "Yuck! What's that?" Will exclaimed with his usual smile.

"It's a birthday cake! What does it look like?"

Will smirked. "It sure doesn't look like a King Karlos Kake. They're oh so descrumptioso!"

Arnold made a face. "Those disgusting little shriveled-up doughball things you get for fifty cents at the candy store? I'd say they're so-so. At best."

"So-so? No! They're oh so de-scrumptioso! I say that right in the commercial."

"Well, this cake is only about a thousand times more de-scrumptioso than any King Karlos Kake you ever tasted. Here." He handed a plateful to Will.

Will picked up the cake and looked at it suspiciously. "I don't know. I've never heard of this cake."

"What do you mean, you've never heard of it?"

"I mean, it's never been in any commercial I know about."

"So?"

"If it's not in a commercial, how can you tell if it's any good?"

Arnold had never met anybody quite as strange as this. "You're weird, you know that?"

"Weird?" Will looked thoughtful. "Oh, yeah! I remember. Somebody called me that once when I had to wear some ugly glasses. But when I took them off and put on AmazingSpecs, everybody started saying I was cool."

Arnold sighed. "I wish everything were that easy!"

"It is easy!" Will grinned. "As easy as pie! As easy as ABC! I bet I've said that a thousand times."

"Yeah? Well, if everything's so easy, tell me how I'm going to fix the busted TV set before my parents find out."

"Call Dweevil's TVville. Prompt repair. Free loaner. Money back if not delighted."

"Oh, sure. Do you have any money?"

Will's grin looked slightly puzzled.

"You know," Arnold said. "Dollars. Cents. Cash."

Will brightened. "Find yourself in need of cash? At Cashline we'll lend it to you in a flash!" he sang.

"Come on!" Arnold scoffed. "They're not going to lend money to a kid!"

Will sang: "The number's toll free, and I'm here to say, you can get cash twenty-four hours a day!"

Arnold scowled, but he picked up the kitchen phone and dialed the toll-free number Will sang next. He was sure it wouldn't work, but he figured there wasn't much harm in trying.

"Cashline!" said a woman's voice over the phone. "For cash in a flash!"

"That's what I need, all right," Arnold said.

"How much would you like?" asked the woman.

"Enough to fix a TV set," Arnold replied.

"Our minimum amount is two hundred dollars."

"Great!" said Arnold. "I guess that ought to be enough." Will flashed him a big wink and an I-told-you-so look.

"Fine," said the voice on the phone. "All you have to do is answer a few simple questions."

"Shoot," said Arnold.

"Name?"

"Arnold Schlemp."

"Middle initial?"

"P."

"Address?"

Arnold spelled it out.

"Birthdate?" asked the woman.

"Today," Arnold said proudly. "I'm twelve."

"Excuse me. We must have a bad connection. I thought you said you were twelve."

"I did say I'm twelve," Arnold said.

"Call us back in nine years, kid." The next thing Arnold heard was a click. He shook his head and hung up.

"See?" said Will, beaming. "Cash in a flash!"

"No cash at all!" Arnold shouted. "They don't lend money to kids. I knew it would never work!"

"Maybe you did something wrong," Will said.

"Maybe everything works right in those commercials of yours. Around here, it's not that easy."

"Of course it's easy. There's an easy solution for everything! Everything!"

"Yeah? What's the solution to fixing my TV? And what am I going to do about you?"

"Me? What do you mean?"

32

"I mean, where are you going to sleep? And eat?"

"Right here."

"Sure, for tonight. Tomorrow I'll have to kick you out."

"But you're my special friend!"

"Don't start that again. My parents have a rule. No sleeping over two nights in a row. And never on school nights. So I don't think they'd be real happy about having an extra kid sleep over every single night of the week. Not to mention feeding you and stuff. We've got to get you back where you came from somehow."

"Why didn't you say so?" said Will. "Nothing to it. Easy as falling off a log."

Arnold scowled. "Really?"

"Really!" said Will. "Come on. I'll show you."

Will led Arnold back to the living room and the broken TV set. Glass was scattered all over the floor. "We'll fix everything right this minute," he said. "Instantly. In a jiffy. You watch. I'll be gone, your TV will be fixed, and nobody will know the difference."

"I don't believe it," Arnold said.

"You'll be amazed!" Will insisted.

"I sure will," Arnold replied.

Will stood in front of the TV set, away from

the glass. He whirled, jumped, and shouted, "Just like magic! It's better than new!"

"Not so loud," Arnold said. The last thing he needed right now was for his parents to come downstairs.

They didn't. But nothing else happened, either.

"Wait a minute," Will said with a baffled expression. "Maybe I have to spin the other way." He whirled, jumped, and shouted, "Just like magic! Better than new!"

"Shhh," Arnold said. But nothing happened.

Nothing at all. The TV set was every bit as broken as it had been ten minutes before. "I'm not exactly amazed," Arnold pointed out.

Will shook his head. "Wow! Things really *are* different around here. That would have worked like a charm where I come from."

Arnold sighed. "Well, I have a plan of my own."

"Hey! Maybe if *you* dance and sing in front of the set . . ."

Arnold shook his head. "Forget it. My plan is to clean up all this glass. Then we can take the TV down to the basement and put it out of sight. Maybe if we're real lucky, my parents won't notice it for a while. Come on. Give me a hand."

Will applauded. Arnold scowled at him and began cleaning up the mess.

Will helped—in his own way. He insisted the fastest way to clean anything up was to point your finger at the mess and say the name of some famous national brand of cleaning product. But every time he tried it, it didn't work at all.

When Arnold turned on the vacuum cleaner, Will complained about how loud it was. He said every vacuum cleaner he had ever heard of played snappy music while it worked.

When it came time to help carry the TV set downstairs, Will grunted and groaned under the weight. He said everything he ever had to lift was light as a feather.

Down in the basement, Will and Arnold set the TV in a corner. Then Arnold found his sleeping bag. It was covered with dust.

"Don't you have a new one? A clean one?" Will demanded.

Arnold was beginning to lose his patience. "Is everything new where you come from?"

Will nodded. "You bet. The only time we have old things around is when we need them to show how wonderful our cleaners are. You know—'Mr. Shine makes things spotless.' He just jumps out of the bottle and sponges away grease and grime while the whole family sings and dances."

"Ha!" Arnold laughed. "My dad was using Mr. Shine to clean the kitchen floor just last week, and believe me, nobody jumped out of the

35

bottle to help. And Dad wasn't exactly singing or dancing while he sponged away that grease and grime."

"He must have been doing something wrong," said Will. "It always works fine where I come from. Always. Every time."

"You know," said Arnold, wiping the sweat from his brow, "where you come from is beginning to sound pretty good to me."

8

"**O**w!" Upstairs in the bathroom, Will threw his towel to the floor. "It's all scratchy!"

"It's just like all our other towels," Arnold told him.

"That's the trouble around here, Arnold. You *need* stuff."

"Like what?"

"Like SuperSof fabric softener, the softener that softens softer." Will picked up the towel and shook his head.

Then he noticed the tube of toothpaste and drew back in horror. "I can't believe it! You don't use Bananadent, the toothpaste with tropical appeal?"

"'Fraid not," said Arnold. "Here. I found you a spare toothbrush."

Will inspected the name on the handle. "I

never heard of this, either. I bet it'll make my teeth fall out."

"Will you brush your teeth before my parents come out and start complaining? It's way past bedtime, and my parents are going to start getting weird."

"Okay, okay. I guess one time won't hurt." Will shrugged as he squeezed the toothpaste onto the toothbrush. Then he smiled his very widest smile at the mirror and practiced smiling wider.

"Hurry up," Arnold said. "Don't mess around."

Arnold went into the bedroom, flopped down on his bed, and stared at the ceiling. This birthday was getting out of hand. What was going to happen once his parents found out about the TV set was not a happy birthday thought. And neither was Will. In a way, Will was sort of like an extra present—the kind you want to send back.

Will finally came into the bedroom. "How do you work this thing?" he asked.

"The sleeping bag? Just get inside," Arnold said.

"What do you mean, get inside?"

"Just climb in."

Will did. Arnold turned out the lamp beside his bed. "Now what?" Will asked.

"Now what what?"

"How are you supposed to sleep in this?"

Arnold sighed. "You close your eyes. Is that too hard for you?"

Will sat up. "This floor's too hard for me. I can't get a peaceful night's sleep down here. I'm used to my SkyBed. It's like sleeping on a cloud."

"Yeah, I've seen the ads," said Arnold. "But we don't have any SkyBeds here. Or clouds, either. Just go to sleep."

"Your bed looks a whole lot more comfortable than this dusty old thing."

"Stop complaining and go to sleep."

"I could, if I had something good to sleep on."

Arnold made a face that Will couldn't see in the dark. "If I sleep in the sleeping bag and let you sleep in my bed, will you quit bothering me?"

"You bet!"

Arnold turned on the light and tumbled out of bed. "Okay, okay. You win."

Will wriggled out of the sleeping bag and bounced into Arnold's bed. "Now, that's more like it," he said with his usual smile.

"Good," Arnold replied as he got into the sleeping bag. "Now turn out the light."

Will did. Arnold curled up and made himself comfortable. In a way, he almost liked the sleeping bag better than his own bed. It reminded him of summer camp. He was almost dreaming when Will said, "I still can't sleep."

"What's wrong now?" Arnold demanded.

"It's better," Will said. "But . . . well, it's just not like sleeping on a cloud."

Arnold grimaced. "Right. It's like sleeping on a bed."

"But that's not the same. It's old-fashioned. Out of date."

"Will you just shut your eyes and go to sleep? Please?"

"I'll try. But I know I'm not going to have a night of angel-filled dreams like on a SkyBed."

"Maybe not," Arnold replied. "But I know what you are going to have if I don't get some sleep."

He rolled over. He noticed Will's Helicopter Shoes glowing in the dark—and his own. An hour ago just knowing they were there would have brought a smile to his face. But now they only reminded him of the broken TV set that he'd have to explain to his parents and this weird kid who was beginning to get on his nerves—and everything else that had happened on this crazy birthday.

Arnold almost wished he'd never heard of Helicopter Shoes. He pulled the flap of the sleeping bag over his head. The dust made him sneeze.

"For the biggest of sneezes, it's Snifflex that pleases," said Will.

Arnold grunted and rolled over. He almost wished he'd never heard of television.

9

"**G**et up, you two," Arnold's mother shouted from the hallway. "You'll be late for school!"

Arnold sleepily pushed back the flap of the sleeping bag. "Good morning!" chirped Will, bright, lively, and already dressed—in Arnold's newest pants and shirt.

"Hey!" Arnold said. "Those are *my* clothes!"

"At least these aren't superterrible," Will replied. "Most of the stuff in your closet is really crummy. It doesn't even have designer labels. And you must've worn everything a million times."

"Who said you could wear my stuff?"

"You don't expect me to wear the same clothes two days in a row, do you? That's just not cool."

"At least you could have asked."

"Arnold, I've been looking around. Most of the stuff you've got here is really pretty crummy. The only things that are any good at all are your UgliBoard and your WaterMusic. Oh, yeah, and that basketball. Everything else is old and worn-out. And you don't have enough of it. You need more."

Arnold sat up. "Yeah? More of what?"

"Just everything, that's all. Things. You need more model planes. You need a computer. You need more games. You need clothes with de-signer labels. You need your own TV and VCR and stereo system and—hey, you need all kinds of stuff!"

"What do I need all that for?"

"You just do, that's all," Will insisted. "Things are what's important. They're what life's all about."

"Arnold!" his father shouted from down-stairs. "Would you mind telling us what you did with the TV set?"

Those were the words Arnold had been dreading. "I can't hear you!" he hollered back.

"See? Your dad knows what's important. You broke one of his things."

"Don't say a word," Arnold told Will as he heard his father hurry up the stairs. "Not even a whisper. Just be quiet. Understand?"

Will nodded. Then Mr. Schlemp burst

through the door. "Arnold, what happened to the TV set?"

Arnold stammered. "We, uh, moved it."

"With Muscleman Movers, you get a moving experience," Will said with a grin. Arnold scowled at him.

So did Arnold's father. "It's too early in the morning for commercials, Will. Now, Arnold, would you mind telling me where you put the TV?"

"The basement," Arnold said.

"An excellent place for it," Arnold's father replied sarcastically. "And I'm sure there was an excellent reason."

Arnold nodded.

"Good," replied Mr. Schlemp, tapping his foot impatiently.

"It's broken," Arnold mumbled.

"What's wrong with it?" his father inquired.

Arnold stared at the floor. "Uh, no picture," he muttered. "No sound, either."

"Were you fooling around with the controls?"

"No," Arnold said. "Honest."

"He threw his shoe at it," Will explained with a big grin. Arnold wanted to throw a shoe at *him*.

"You threw your shoe at it?" Arnold's father

shouted at Arnold. "Why would you do a thing like that?"

Arnold felt about one inch tall. "It's a long story."

"I love long stories," his father said impatiently.

"My Helicopter shoe broke?" Arnold squeaked.

"Your insanely expensive new present from Grandma? You broke that already?"

"*I* didn't break it," Arnold explained. "It broke itself. The tongue just fell out. See?" He picked up the ruined shoe and held it out to his father.

Mr. Schlemp looked at it. "And you expected to fix this shoe by breaking our TV set?"

Arnold sighed. "I was kind of frustrated."

"Breakfast at McDill's will get you going in the morning!" Will sang happily.

"Would you please be quiet for a minute?" Mr. Schlemp interrupted. "I've got problems enough with one young man around here."

Will nodded with a pleasant smirk. Mr. Schlemp turned back to Arnold. "Now, let me get this straight. You threw your shoe, and that broke the TV set?"

"Sort of," Arnold mumbled.

"Exactly what broke?"

"The screen," Arnold muttered in his quietest voice. "It just kind of shattered."

"So *that* was the noise we heard last night!" Mr. Schlemp said with a stern look on his face.

Arnold stared at his toes and mumbled, "Yes." He waited to hear what his father would say next. But his father didn't say anything.

Arnold looked up. "Am I going to get punished for this?"

"Of course," said Mr. Schlemp. "I just haven't decided how yet."

"He didn't mean to break the TV," Will remarked.

"I'm sure he didn't," replied Mr. Schlemp.

"It was an accident," Arnold said. "I never dreamed the TV would break. I was hardly even aiming at it."

"I can tell you one thing, Arnold. You won't be watching any TV this week. And possibly next week. And probably not all that much the week after that."

Arnold didn't say a word. The way things were going, he thought he might be happy if he never saw another TV set as long as he lived.

"And if I were you," his father went on, "I would not make any major spending plans involving your allowance."

Arnold just nodded. Right now he didn't

care if he ever bought a single new thing in his entire life.

"Now get ready for school," Mr. Schlemp ordered. "You don't want to be late."

"We won't be late," said Will. "Not with my BeeperWatch, the watch that keeps you beepably prompt."

"Good to hear it," Mr. Schlemp muttered, and stormed out of the room.

"You see?" said Will. "If you had another four or five TV sets, your father would probably never have missed this one. You definitely need more. Of everything."

Arnold wasn't so sure about that. But he definitely knew a few people and things he could use less of.

10

Eddie Magistretti came out his front door and looked down at Arnold's feet. Then he noticed Will's outfit. "Arnold, did this guy rob you at gunpoint and make you give up your clothes, or what?"

"Hi! Delighted to meet you!" said Will, extending his hand.

Eddie looked at it suspiciously. "Arnold, who is this kid?"

"You're not going to believe it when I tell you," Arnold replied.

"Come on! Shake hands and join the fun!" Will boomed.

"This guy's a little too friendly," Eddie told Arnold. "Does he have one of those buzzer things that's going to zap me if I shake with him?"

"Let's be special friends!" Will suggested.

"Is he weird, or what?" Eddie demanded. "Arnold, if this is some kind of joke, all I can say is, watch out."

"It's a bigger joke than you think," Arnold moaned.

Eddie drew his hand back. "What are you talking about?"

"I'm telling you, you're not going to believe it!" Arnold repeated.

"Yes, it's unbelievable, but it's true!" Will fingered Eddie's collar and peeked inside. "You've got dirt-around-the-neck. Dirt-around-the-neck!"

Eddie made a fist. "I am going to give you some dirt-around-the-neck in about fifteen seconds if you don't let go of me, buster."

Will shrugged and moved away. "One wash with Tweet, and your clothes'll be clean as a whistle!"

"What's the gag?" Eddie demanded. "Is he some relative of yours or something?"

Arnold shook his head. "Worse. This kid came through my TV set."

"You don't expect me to believe that!" Eddie said.

"See? I told you you wouldn't," Arnold replied. "But maybe you will when you hear everything else that happened."

Eddie made a face, but he listened very seriously to the rest of Arnold's story. "Look," he said when Arnold was through. "We're supposed to be best friends. This is serious. I want the truth, or we're not going to be best friends anymore."

"Every word I told you is true," Arnold said sadly. "He came from the TV set just the way I said he did, and I don't know how to send him back."

Eddie stared at Will. "Boy! It's like he's some sort of alien. On the wrong planet. If he's not careful, he could get himself in a lot of trouble." Eddie looked thoughtful. "And maybe you, too, Arnold. What are you going to do with him?"

"I don't know. Could he sleep over at your place tonight till we figure something out?"

"Are you kidding? This guy? He'd probably insult my parents—you know, tell them they had perspiration odor or something. And on a school night? Forget it!"

"I thought you just said we were best friends," Arnold replied.

"I did. But I can't even have *you* sleep over on a school night—let alone this weird guy."

"Hey! Wait up!" Ellen Belitzky was just coming out her front door.

"Uh-oh," Arnold whispered to Eddie. "Should we tell her?"

"Not a chance," Eddie whispered back. "Even if we did, she's so stuck-up she wouldn't believe us. She'd just make us the laughingstock of the school, that's all!"

"Well, what are we going to tell her, then?" Arnold demanded.

Eddie thought fast. "Say he's your cousin. From Cleveland." He turned to Will. "You're Arnold's cousin. From Cleveland. Got that?"

Will grinned and nodded.

"Who's this cute guy?" Ellen asked.

Will smiled his widest. "Will Flack. Delighted to meet you."

"Are you new around here?"

"He's my cousin," Arnold said. "He's visiting."

"Pleased to meet you," said Ellen. "Where are you from?"

"He's from Cleveland," Arnold said quickly, before Will could go into one of his song-and-dance routines.

"What's it like where you come from?" Ellen inquired.

Will laughed. "A lot better than here!"

Ellen scowled. "Better? What's better about it?"

"Just everything, that's all," said Will. "Where I come from everything's clean."

"Everything's clean here," said Ellen.

"No, it isn't. Eddie has dirt-around-the-neck."

Ellen giggled.

"That was so funny I forgot to laugh," Eddie growled.

"And where I come from, everybody's happy," said Will. "We walk around singing and dancing."

"So do we, sometimes," said Ellen.

"But we do it all day long," said Will. He whirled around and broke into his Helicopter Shoes routine. "And we wouldn't even think of wearing drippy no-name shoes like yours."

"These are very expensive shoes," Ellen sniffed. "I really don't care what you think of them."

Eddie laughed. "Sure, you do. Just last week you gave us a big hassle because your expensive new shirt had some dumb little porcupine on it and ours didn't."

"That's different," Ellen sniffed. "Porcupine shirts are in style. Nobody cares about Helicopter Shoes."

"Hey, that ugly house you came from needs StormStopper siding," Will added cheerfully. "With StormStopper siding, your home will look and feel its best."

"What a nerve!" Ellen exclaimed. "First he

insults our neighborhood. Then he insults my shoes. Now he insults my house. You know what, Will Flack? I take it back! You're not cute at all! You're perfectly obnoxious! And so are your friends!" She stuck her nose in the air and ran across the street.

Eddie and Arnold laughed so hard they nearly fell down. "You know," Eddie said, "maybe this guy isn't so bad after all." He stuck his hand out toward Will.

But instead of shaking Eddie's hand, Will just stared at it. "Those fingernails are filthy!" he exclaimed. "You need NailKleen from Nailco."

Eddie yanked his hand away and shook his head sadly. "Just like I said before, Arnold. You definitely have a problem here."

11

As he walked through the front door of Snuffy Snortburger Memorial Public School, Arnold discovered his "cousin" had never heard of homework. Or homerooms. Or schoolbooks. Or classes.

"What *do* you do all day?" Eddie asked.

"Sing and dance and talk about neat stuff," Will replied.

"You don't go to school?" Arnold asked.

Will shook his head.

"Not ever?" Eddie demanded.

"Only when I'm in a school kind of commercial. Like the one where all us kids and the teachers dance on the desks and munch candy bars while we sing about Carmelona, the sweet treat with the crunchy nut surprise."

"Well, don't do any dancing in class around

here," said Arnold. "And don't eat candy, either. Just watch me and do what I do."

Eddie grinned. "And don't say anything about some of the teachers' breath—or believe me, you'll wish you hadn't."

Will looked surprised. "Don't you think they ought to know?"

"Yes," Arnold admitted. "But it's not polite to tell them."

"Not polite?" Will said. "Where I come from, if you tell somebody about how to fix bad breath, the next thing you know, the person is laughing and smiling."

"Not here," Eddie said. "Here people get insulted."

Will sighed. "This really is a strange place, all right."

"This is my cousin," Arnold told his homeroom teacher, Miss Garelick. "His name is Will Flack. He's from Cleveland."

"Pleased to meet you, Will," Miss Garelick said.

"You know, you have beautiful lips," said Will. "It must be Kissable, the lipstick with the golden glow."

Miss Garelick gave him a frosty scowl. "I hope you enjoy our school."

"Me, too," Will said. "I've only been to

school a couple of times before. But I promise I won't eat candy."

"He means he's never been to *public* school," Arnold added quickly. "He goes to private school."

"Will, he can sit in the back of the room," said Miss Garelick. "And you can sit with him instead of in your regular place. But no talking!"

"What about singing?" Will asked.

"I visited his school once," Arnold broke in. "They have music class every day first thing in the morning. It's kind of weird."

"We don't have music class scheduled for today," said Miss Garelick matter-of-factly. "Now, take your seats."

"Where should we take them?" Will asked very seriously.

Miss Garelick sighed. "Apparently they teach stale old jokes in private school."

"Come on," Arnold said, dragging Will by the arm. "Visitors should be seen and not heard."

But the rest of that day the visitor was seen and heard a little more than Arnold had in mind. When Miss Garelick called the roll and Arnold answered "here," so did Will. Miss Garelick just ignored him, even though the class giggled. But when she asked who knew how many pints were in a gallon and Arnold raised his hand, Will did, too.

"Our visitor's hand is up. Will, do you know the answer?"

"Answer? What answer?" said Will. The class giggled again.

"The answer to my question about how many pints are in a gallon," Miss Garelick explained patiently.

"Huh?" Will said.

"Why did you put your hand up?" Miss Garelick asked.

Will smiled his smile. "Because Arnold did."

More giggling from the class. Arnold rolled his eyes in dismay. "Thank you, Will," said Miss Garelick, "but I'd appreciate it if you'd stop your clowning."

"Clowning?" Will said, bewildered.

"Never mind," said Miss Garelick. She called on Arnold. "Eight," he answered. Then Will repeated the exact same word.

"Thank you," said Miss Garelick sternly. "One more humorous remark and you will have an opportunity to meet our principal."

Arnold turned to Will. "Quiet!" he whispered. "You're going to get us both in trouble."

"I was just doing what you did," Will whispered back. "That's what you said to do."

"Okay. Fine. But for now just be quiet. Don't say anything. Nothing at all."

Will folded his arms across his chest and maintained a silent grin the rest of the morning. "You nearly got in trouble for a minute there," Eddie told him at lunchtime. "So what do you think of school?"

"Can I talk now?" Will asked.

"Sure," Arnold told him.

"Well, this school just isn't cool," Will said with a laugh. "Not at all. When we go to school in one of my commercials, we play with SuperStuff, the plastic putty that can be anything you want. We toss it around the class while we sing and laugh."

"Some school!" Eddie grunted through a mouthful of baloney.

"Or run around the playground in our WoverAlls," Will went on. "And all the kids in my schools are good-looking, and everybody wears neat new clothes. These kids look doofy. And their clothes are the pits."

"Everybody can't be handsome and beautiful and wear expensive clothes all the time," Arnold said. "What's so terrible about that?"

"Not cool, that's all. Not cool." Will scowled at his sandwich. "And by the way, this peanut butter isn't great, either. It's nowhere near as good as Chunkeroo, the peanut butter with the giant chunks of flavor."

Arnold peeled his bread apart and looked. "It is Chunkeroo. That's the kind my mom always buys."

Will snorted. "If this were Chunkeroo, every bite would make me feel peanuterrific!" He took a bite. "I sure don't feel peanuterrific."

Eddie made a face. "Fine. You want to trade for half a baloney sandwich?"

"Is it Pony baloney, the unphony baloney?" Will asked.

"Baloney's baloney!" said Eddie.

"Pony baloney's unphony baloney!" Will sang. "It's tony baloney, not bony baloney!"

"Forget I ever offered," Eddie said. "I know baloney when I hear it!"

Late that afternoon Miss Garelick led a spelling bee. Will's first word was "butter." He couldn't spell it at all—not even the "b." He just kept his mouth shut, even when he heard a bunch of giggles from the rest of the class.

Then Miss Garelick asked Cynthia, "How do you spell 'remedy'?"

Will shot to his feet and announced, "I spell it H-E-A-D-A-C-H-E-R-I-N. Your pain will be gone in seconds!"

The class howled. Arnold wanted to hide beneath his desk. "All right, Will," said Miss Garelick with a frown. "That's enough of your humor, please."

But when Cynthia spelled "R-E-M-E-D-Y," and Miss Garelick said, "Correct," Will shot to his feet.

"That's *not* correct," he insisted. "You spell 'remedy' H-E-A-D-A-C-H-E-R-I-N and everybody knows it."

Miss Garelick looked furious. "Is that what they teach you in private school?"

"Everybody knows that," said Will. "It's not fair to let her spell it some other way."

"Excuse me for a moment, class. Arnold and Will, would you follow me, please?"

Arnold shot Will a fierce look. But Will just grinned, whispered, "I'm telling you, she's wrong," and followed him out the door.

"Now look, you two," said Miss Garelick. "I don't mind visitors. But we can't have Will disrupting the class this way. Any more outbursts, and I'll have to send you both to the principal's office." She turned to Will. "You do know what the principal's office is, don't you?"

"No," said Will, shaking his head and smiling his most irritating smile. "Not me. I've never heard of it before."

"One more crack out of you, young man, and you'll see it for yourself."

"Maybe they don't have a principal's office in his private school," Arnold suggested.

"Honest," said Will. "I don't even know what a principal is."

"Well, you're going to find out right now," said Miss Garelick. "Arnold, you certainly know what a principal is. And where."

"Yes, Miss Garelick," Arnold said wearily. She reached inside, handed him two hall passes, went back inside, and shut the door.

"What is a principal, anyhow?" Will asked.

Arnold just rolled his eyes and sighed. Will looked like any normal human being. But Eddie was right. Will was an alien, all right. From the Planet of No School.

12

Eddie caught up with Arnold and Will after school. "Hey!" he shouted. "What happened in Mrs. Nofziger's office?"

"Nothing much," said Arnold, rolling his eyes. "He just told Mrs. Nofziger that her face needed plastic surgery. That's all."

Eddie giggled at the thought. "Nice going!" he said, patting Will on the back.

"I was only trying to help," Will replied. "But that always seems to get me in trouble."

"Amazing!" Eddie laughed. "What did she do?"

"Kicked us out," Arnold said. "Told us that he couldn't ever come back to this school again. Ever."

"Well, at least she didn't make you spell the word 'remedy' on the blackboard eight hundred times or something," Eddie replied.

"We were lucky, all right," Arnold agreed. "It could've been a whole lot worse. But what are we going to do now?"

"About what?"

"About you know who. You have any bright ideas about how to send him home?"

"Take Busway Lines. It gets you there! On the dot, fair and square!" Will piped up.

"Somehow, I don't think the bus is going to get you where you want to go," Eddie remarked.

"Right," Arnold agreed. "So we've got to figure something out. You sure he can't stay at your place just for tonight?"

"Well, we can go by my house and try," Eddie offered. "But I know what my dad is going to say."

"Um-diddle-super!" Will chirped.

"Not exactly," said Eddie.

Ten minutes later Eddie came out of his house shaking his head. "What *did* he say?" Arnold asked.

"Stuff that I don't think somebody from inside the TV set ought to learn. They don't use that kind of language on TV."

"No, huh?"

"Um-diddle-triple No with double-fudge Never sauce on it," said Eddie.

"What now?" Arnold asked.

"Well," said Eddie, "we could go back to

your place and goof around while we try to think of something."

"Bo-ring," said Will. "Dullsville. Square city."

"How about the mall?" Arnold suggested.

"How is going to the mall going to help this guy?" Eddie snorted.

Arnold looked thoughtful. "I don't know. Maybe we can sneak him in someplace and have him live there overnight like in this book I read. Maybe on the way over we'll figure something out."

"Yeah, who knows?" said Eddie. "Maybe somebody'll hire him as a salesman. He's sure got plenty of experience."

Halfway to the mall Will said, "Wait a second."

Arnold and Eddie stopped in their tracks. Will unlaced one of his Helicopter Shoes and took it off.

"What are you doing?" Arnold asked.

"It feels funny," Will said with a look of pain that twisted his smile. "It almost"—Will searched for the word—"hurts."

"Hurts?" Eddie scoffed. "A shoe that costs six times as much as any other shoe, and it hurts? I don't believe it!"

"Believe it," Arnold said.

Will took off his sock. "Wow!" Eddie exclaimed. "No wonder it hurts. That's the biggest blister I ever saw."

"Next to the one I got from my Helicopter Shoes yesterday," Arnold noted.

"The biggest what?" Will asked.

"Blister," Eddie replied. "That big red disgusting bubbly oozy thing on your heel. Don't people get blisters where you come from?"

Will looked as if he was thinking hard. "Bunions, calluses, corns, or blisters? Spray on some FootFixer, misses and misters!" he sang without dancing. "Is this what a blister is?"

"Sure is," Eddie said.

"Then all I need is some FootFixer," Will said.

"I keep telling you, it's not that easy here," said Arnold. "You can't pick up a can of something and expect it to solve your problems, just like that!"

"Sure I can!" Will insisted. "And I'm not moving another step until I get some."

As he flopped down in the middle of the sidewalk, his smile faded just a tiny bit. "It's hot out here. I'm tired. I'm thirsty. I need a lift."

Arnold and Eddie looked at each other and smirked. They knew just what commercial Will was quoting now. "He must think the ColdPops man is going to drive up right beside him," Eddie whispered to Arnold.

"Right, and hand him an IcyJuicy," Arnold whispered back. "Just like that."

"Boy, is he ever in for a surprise," Eddie whispered. "I almost feel sorry for him. Even if he is kind of obnoxious."

"I'm tired! I'm thirsty! I need a lift!" Will repeated a little louder.

"Forget it, Will," Arnold said sympathetically. "That won't work here."

"I bet it would work just fine where you come from, right?" Eddie asked.

"Number one," said Will, counting things off on his fingers, "it wouldn't be this hot where I come from. We all use Eskimo air conditioners, the units with Igloo Power. Number two, if it was hot, everybody would be hanging around the swimming pool drinking a nice cool Lemonorama, the soft drink with that citrussuper taste. Number three, nobody would be crazy enough to walk this far. If you have to go anywhere far, you drive in a brand-new car or Whizmobile van, the van what am. And if things got really bad, all you would have to say is 'I'm tired. I'm thirsty. I need a lift,' and the ColdPops man would come to your rescue."

Just then a faint tinkly tune wafted through the air. "I don't believe it!" Eddie exclaimed.

"We must be hearing things," Arnold agreed.

66

But the very next second the ColdPops truck came around the corner playing its tinkly tune. "See?" Will said proudly, waving at the ColdPops man.

The truck pulled up beside them. "What'll it be?" asked the ColdPops man, just like in the TV commercials.

"Be careful," Eddie whispered to Arnold. "Maybe something happened somehow and we got transported to where Will comes from."

Arnold and Eddie watched suspiciously as Will ordered a IcyJuicy and the ColdPops man handed it to him—just like in the commercial. Will unwrapped it, took one lick, and started dancing—just like in the commercial.

But what happened next wasn't like the commercial at all. "Ow!" Will shouted as he landed on his blister.

"Enough with the dancing, pal," said the ColdPops man. "How about my seventy-five cents?"

"Seventy-five what?" Will asked. Eddie and Arnold giggled.

The ColdPops man looked impatient. "Seventy-five you know darned well what. Three quarters. Seven dimes and a nickel."

"I don't have any quarters," Will said. "I've never even seen a nickel."

The ColdPops man stepped out of his truck

and grabbed Will by the collar of his borrowed shirt. "You'd better pay me," he threatened, "and you'd better be quick about it."

"I don't know what you're talking about," Will said. "Honest!"

"We'd better help him," Arnold told Eddie. "I don't think he's had much experience with money."

"Or threats, either," Eddie added. "People hardly ever get mad in commercials."

"We'll pay for him," Arnold told the Cold-Pops man. "He must've forgotten his money."

"Forgot, humph!" said the ColdPops man as Arnold dug seventy-five cents from his pocket. "He was trying to steal that IcyJuicy from me."

"'Steal'?" Will said. "What does that mean?"

"You know darned well what that means, buddy," said the ColdPops man.

"I don't think he does," Eddie said. "Really. He's not from around here. He's from a whole different place."

"Where's that, bud?" asked the ColdPops man, cooling down.

"Cleveland!" Eddie and Arnold shouted together.

"I guess that might explain it," said the ColdPops man. He scratched his head as he got back into his truck. "Maybe."

13

"**M**an, that was close!" Eddie told Will. "You could've gotten arrested or something. Don't you know about money?"

"Sure, I *know* about it. Cash in a flash. That kind of thing. But I don't understand why anybody needs it."

Eddie made a face. "You need it to buy stuff."

"We don't. We get all our clothes and food and stuff for free."

"Well, it doesn't work that way here," Arnold informed him. "If you want something that's not yours, you have to pay for it."

"I want plenty," said Will. "Let's get some of this money."

"You don't just *get* it," Arnold said. "You have to earn it."

"How?"

"By working," Arnold explained.

"Like at a job," Eddie added.

Will gave them a blank look. "Job?"

"You know," Arnold said. "Washing cars. Cooking hamburgers. Stuff like that."

Will looked thoughtful. "What about that homework you were talking about? That's work, right?"

Arnold nodded.

"So you get money for that?" Will asked.

Eddie laughed. "It doesn't work that way."

"That's no fair."

Arnold and Eddie looked at each other and grinned. "It sure isn't," Arnold said.

"That's for sure," Eddie agreed. "Come on, let's get moving, or we'll never get to the mall."

They started on their way. But Will complained about his blister with every step he took.

"I thought those are supposed to be such great shoes," Eddie said. "How come they're hurting your feet?"

"Probably because they're all worn-out," said Will.

"But they're brand-new!" Arnold said.

"You call these brand-new? Are you kidding? They're all beat up! They've even got little scuffs on the sides. I've worn these shoes longer than any pair I've had in my entire life. Every time I'm in a commercial, I get a *really* brand-new pair. That's why they always look so bright and shiny."

Eddie looked down at Will's shoes. "You want to swap awhile?"

"I'm not going to wear those doofy scuffed-up holey old things," Will said.

"I'll bet they're a lot more comfortable than what you're wearing," Eddie said.

"These have bounce-gas soles," Will reminded him.

"I know all about 'em," Eddie replied. "Suit yourself. If you want to whine every time you take a step, it's fine with me."

Will looked thoughtful. "Okay. It's a deal. For a little while, anyway."

They sat down and traded shoes. Eddie stood up and tried out the bounce-gas soles. "Not bad," he said. "Nice to find somebody with feet as big as mine. How do those feel?"

Will stood up and took a couple of steps. "Okay, I guess. I just hope nobody laughs at me in them."

"Hasn't ever happened to me," Eddie assured him. "And I bet it never will."

"How much farther?" Will demanded.

Eddie pointed. "That's the mall down there."

"Where?"

Arnold stuck out his arm. "There. Straight ahead. See?"

"All I see is a big ugly parking lot."

"That's it," Eddie said. "The stores are in that big building in the middle."

"You mean you dragged me all this way in this terrible heat just to see some big ugly parking lot with a big ugly building in the middle of it?"

"This guy is getting on my nerves," Eddie whispered to Arnold.

"Mine, too," Arnold agreed. "But we can't just let him run around on his own. He doesn't know anything about anything. He'll just get into trouble."

"He sure is a pain," Eddie said. "But I guess in a way you're sort of responsible for him. After all, he did come through your TV set when you broke it."

"Don't remind me," Arnold replied.

"Besides," Eddie added, "I've only been wearing these shoes for about half a minute, and it already feels like *I'm* getting a blister."

"Told you so," said Arnold.

14

"**A**t last!" Will whooped as he came through the mall entranceway. "Cool air!"

"Don't be so dramatic," Eddie told him.

But Will had perked up again. To the left and right, ahead and behind, were dozens of stores, every one twinkling with a "buy me" gleam. The Snafflefield Mall had just about everything you could think of. Will kept whirling around to take it all in.

"Wow!" he cried. "It's amazing! It's stupendous! It's unbelievable!"

"If you think this is good, you ought to see the mall over in Wartburg," Eddie said. "They've got a waterfall and trees and a merry-go-round and everything."

"It's spectacular here!" Will went on. "It's flabbergasting! It's almost like where I come from!"

Arnold was astounded. "Where you come from is like this?"

"Sure!" Will said as he kept twirling and looking around. "It's all air-conditioned like this! And look at all the neat stuff! Everything's brand-new here—just like at home!"

"I can't believe it!" Eddie exclaimed. "You live in a shopping mall?"

"Well, sort of. I mean, we have houses and everything. But they're right outside. You never ever have to walk in the heat. Hey, look at that!"

Right in the middle of the mall was a shiny brand-new red-and-black sports car under a big sign that said WIN! It was the prize in a contest at Mergenthaler's Department Store. "Now, that's what I call a car," said Will. "Not a scratch on it! No dirt, either. Why didn't you tell me about this place before?"

"Lucky you," Eddie whispered to Arnold. "He likes this place so much maybe he *would* be willing to stay here."

"Wow!" Will kept saying. "This is living! Look at all this great stuff!" He hurried down the main corridor so fast Arnold and Eddie could hardly keep up with him. But finally he stopped to admire the window of the Shoeperman Shoppe.

"I know, I know," Arnold groaned before

Will could get a word in edgewise. "Helicopter Shoes."

"I've already got Helicopter Shoes," Will pointed out.

"You mean *I've* got them," Eddie reminded him. "And they're starting to hurt. Let's trade back." And he began untying his shoelaces.

"What you need," said Will, "is a pair of these other great shoes in this window. In fact, there's great stuff all over the place here. We should take some back to your house, Arnold."

"With what?" Arnold wanted to know.

"What do you mean?" Will demanded.

"All I've got left is a couple of dollars," Arnold said.

Will just stared blankly.

"It takes money to buy this stuff," Eddie reminded him.

"You're kidding!" Will said.

"Scout's honor," Arnold replied. "See those dollar signs and numbers on those price tags?"

"We don't have price tags where I come from. We just sort of dance in with one thing and dance out with another."

"You do that here," Arnold said, "and you'll get arrested."

"Arrested?" Will looked puzzled.

"Lock you up? Send you to jail?" Eddie demanded, but the look on Will's face said he'd never heard of that, either.

Will shook his head. "Amazing! Unbelievable! We walked all that way, and now we're finally here, and we can't do anything because we don't have any money?"

"We can hang out and look at stuff," Arnold said.

"But we can't take it with us?"

Arnold shook his head.

"That's crazy!" Will shouted. "It's insaner than Crazy Coconutto's prices!"

"It beats school," Arnold pointed out.

Eddie took off one Helicopter shoe and rubbed his aching heel. "Look, I've had it with these things," he told Will. "Come on, let's trade back."

"Fine with me," Will replied. "I'm tired of wearing your doofy—hey, look!" Suddenly he dashed across the mall and disappeared into Video Vic's.

Arnold and Eddie exchanged a worried look. Then they did the only thing they could do: they ran after him. Eddie did the best he could with one shoe off.

As they ran into Video Vic's, Arnold and Eddie heard a familiar tune. On the dozen screens there was the Helicopter Shoes commercial:

We're talking
Helicopter
Helicopter
Helicopter Shoes.

Inside, Will was staring at a wall of TV sets. Arnold and Eddie ran up to him.

"Hey! Where am I?" he demanded without taking his eyes off the screens.

My shoes are the best
And that's the truth.
You gotta move with the 'Copter
Or else you're uncouth.

"You're right here," said Eddie, rubbing his sore foot. "How about giving me back my shoes?"

Will ignored him. "I mean up there on the screen," he said. "I'm supposed to be right behind Helicopter Jones!"

Without these shoes
I couldn't be great
They're the shoes
That let me levitate.

"Everybody else is there!" Will complained.

"I think you come in right after this part," said Arnold.

Hey, I made the shot
And so will you
As long as you're wearing
My Helicopter shoe.

Then an amazing transformation happened right there in Video Vic's: Will's usual big smile turned into a genuine, unmistakable, no-doubt-about-it frown. "Where?" he demanded. "Everybody else is there, but I'm not! I'm gone! Vanished!"

Helicopter
Helicopter
Helicopter Shoes.

It was true. Where Will had been in the old commercial was just a blank bluish hole—on all twenty-four screens.

"This is no good!" he wailed. "I'm supposed to be there! I'm supposed to be the star!"

Arnold and Eddie couldn't think of anything to say.

"It's no fair! I want to go back!" Will wailed. "I want to go back!" In a fit of anger he grabbed the Helicopter shoe from Eddie's hand and threw it toward the TV sets.

We're talking
Helicopter
Helicopter
Helicopter Shoes . . .

The TV screen closest to the floor shattered with a horrible tinkly crash. It reminded Arnold of what had happened to his TV.

But this time it was different. The TV was behaving like a giant vacuum cleaner. First it sucked in the Helicopter shoe that Will had thrown. Then the suction got so strong that Arnold had to grab onto a shelf to keep his balance.

Finally it stopped. Arnold looked around. Will Flack was still standing right beside him. But Eddie was gone!

"Look!" Will cried, pointing to all the other TV screens. There, on every screen, in bright color, in brand-new Helicopter Shoes, gesturing frantically toward the audience—was Eddie!

15

The regular program started again on all the screens except the broken one. Eddie disappeared from the screen—as he had from the video store, the mall, and real life.

"Did you kids do that?" shouted the clerk, rushing over.

"We didn't do anything!" Arnold lied. "That dumb TV exploded!"

"I had my eye on you. There were three of you when you came in here. Where's your friend?"

"What friend?" Arnold asked.

"The one who smashed my TV!" cried the clerk.

"Nobody smashed your TV!" Will said. "It just blew up!"

"Don't lie to me," the clerk growled.

"I don't know anything about that kid," Arnold lied. "He wasn't with us. He was just sort of hanging out."

"I'm calling the guards," the clerk said. "Don't you move."

But Arnold did move. He moved fast. He dragged Will with him. His old, beat-up shoes and the ones Eddie had swapped didn't stop running until they were out of the mall, across the parking lot, and back in Arnold's neighborhood.

"My feet hurt!" Will cried, slumping in a heap.

"Come on!" Arnold said. "We can't stop now. We have to get Eddie back."

"He's in the commercial now instead of me!" Will moaned. "How are we going to get him back? I might be stuck here for good!"

"I think I know what happened," said Arnold. "We may be able to save him. But we've got to get back to my house fast!"

"What happened? I know what happened! He was wearing my shoes, that's what happened—the shoes from my commercial!"

"Right!" said Arnold. "Almost, anyway. When you threw that shoe and broke the TV, the commercial must have realized you were missing. But Eddie was wearing the other shoe, so things got all confused, and he went back through the TV instead of you."

"I'll never get back! I just know it! I'm stuck here forever with these doofy dumb shoes!"

"Will you come on?" Arnold demanded. "We haven't got time to argue. That commercial's always on just before the five-o'clock news. We've got to get back home by then, or Eddie may be stuck in that commercial till tomorrow, and by then it might be too late. You might be stuck here forever."

"Anything but that!" said Will. "Anything!" On his aching feet he hurried along right behind Arnold.

Back home Arnold checked his watch: there were just five minutes to go. "Put on one of my Helicopter Shoes!" he shouted as they ran upstairs to his room. "And hurry!"

Will took off Eddie's shoes as fast as he could. "Ow!" he said.

"What's the matter now?" Arnold asked.

"That whatchamacallit again."

"The blister? Don't worry. In a minute or two you'll be able to get FootFixer or whatever you need."

"Right, if your plan works. But nothing works around here. Look at this!" He held up the dangling tongue of Arnold's Helicopter shoe.

"Just hang on to the one that's no good. Put on the other one."

Will tried. "I can't lace it up! I can't even get into this shoe. It's way too small for me!"

"I forgot about that," Arnold said. "Look, just be sure it's on your foot somehow."

"I don't know . . ." Will muttered. "Hey, wait a second! I can't go back there in these clothes."

Arnold looked at the clothes Will had borrowed from him. "Okay. Change into yours. And hurry up about it."

Will frantically took off Arnold's shirt and pants and changed into his Helicopter Jones outfit. Then he stuffed his foot into Arnold's left Helicopter shoe.

"Come on! Hurry up!" Arnold urged. "Into my parents' room! Quick!"

Will moaned as he limped into the Schlemps' bedroom with Arnold's too tiny left shoe half on and nothing but a Helicopter sock on his other foot. Arnold had already warmed up the TV. All they had to do now was wait. And hope. And worry. What Arnold worried about most was that when this all was over, he might just have *two* broken TV sets to worry about.

"Okay," said Arnold. "In a second or two the commercial is going to come on again—and Eddie's going to be in it."

"That's not news," said Will.

"I know," Arnold told him. "All you have to do is throw your shoe at the TV set. If we're lucky, everything should work out fine. At least until my parents get home. You ready?"

Will held the tongueless shoe in his other hand. "I sure hope this works."

"Just get ready," Arnold said. "Here it comes!"

Helicopter
Helicopter
Helicopter Shoes.

Helicopter
Helicopter
Helicopter Shoes.

"There he is!" Will shouted.

There Eddie was, all right. He had taken off the Helicopter Shoes and was dancing around in his socks.

We're talking
Helicopter
Helicopter
Helicopter Shoes.

"Okay, Will," Arnold said. "Come on! Toss that shoe!"

But Eddie was clowning and making faces and acting like a gorilla. All Will could do was laugh.

Hey, Helicopter here
And I just want to say
My Helicopter Shoes
Are the shoes of today!

You can dance and jump around
In any old shoes.
But mine are the ones
That will cure your blues.

Eddie dangled his head and stuck out his tongue and flapped his hands like big ears. Then he held his nose. Will acted as though it was the funniest thing he'd ever seen.

Helicopter
Helicopter
Helicopter Shoes.

Eddie's antics really were hilarious. "Stop laughing, Will!" Arnold said with a giggle he couldn't help. "Just throw the stupid shoe!"

We're talking
Helicopter

Helicopter
Helicopter Shoes.

"Come on!" Arnold said. "You're going to miss your friends! You're going to miss all your brand-new things! Your blister will never stop hurting!"

Will paid no attention. "We're not allowed to do stuff like that! He's hilarious!"

Arnold grabbed Will and shook him hard. "Come on! Throw it! Just like you did in the video store!"

My shoes are the best
And that's the truth.
You gotta move with the 'Copter
Or else you're uncouth.

Without these shoes
I couldn't be great
They're the shoes
That let me levitate.

Helicopter Jones went up for the shot—but Eddie sneaked up by surprise and stole the ball away from him. Then he spun it around on his head. Will and Arnold collapsed with laughter. Helicopter Jones just looked confused and upset.

Hey, I made the shot
And so will you
As long as you're wearing
My Helicopter shoe.

"You *didn't* make the shot!" Will hollered through his laughter. "You missed! Serves you right!"

Helicopter
Helicopter
Helicopter Shoes.

"Look!" Will pointed. Eddie stuck out his tongue and made faces at the camera and fell down on his rear end.

It was hilarious, all right. But there wasn't much time left. Arnold was positive his plan was going to fail. He would have grabbed the shoe and thrown it himself, but he was afraid that if he did, *he'd* be the one the TV set would suck in.

We're talking
Helicopter . . .

Will was still laughing. There was only one thing to do. Arnold grabbed Will's arm and aimed it at the TV set. The shoe went flying.

Helicopter . . .

The TV suddenly exploded inward with a glassy tinkle.

Helicopter Shoes . . .

Arnold watched Will get sucked up into the set feet first.

We're talking . . .

The song kept echoing through the room. But nothing else happened for a second or two.

Helicopter . . .

The TV gave off a puff of smoke and made another tinkly noise.

Helicopter . . .

Arnold crossed his fingers and hoped hard.

16

The noise stopped. The smoke began to clear. "Boy, was that ever weird!" said Eddie Magistretti in his stocking feet.

"You're back!" Arnold exclaimed.

"Yeah, and am I ever glad!"

"Was it fun?" Arnold asked.

"Fun? Are you kidding?"

"Will kept saying how wonderful it is there."

"Wonderful! Ha! It stinks!"

"Really?" Arnold said.

"Everybody's all stuck-up like Will—or Ellen. When the commercial's not on, all they do is sit around with big smiles on their faces and talk about how good-looking they are and how neat their brand-new stuff is."

"Well, isn't it neat?"

"Sort of. So what? A little dirt never hurt anybody. Those Helicopter Shoes were brand-new, but they were so stiff they hurt like crazy. Give me my good old comfortable broken-in sneaks any day."

"What about all the fun everybody's supposed to have all the time?" Arnold asked.

"Fun? Hey, they *make* you have fun. You can't do anything at all except what you're told. They have people there to tell you to smile and *look* like you're having fun, just to make sure you don't forget. And Will thinks school is boring! At least in school they don't make you smile when there's nothing to smile about!"

"What about Helicopter Jones? Did you get his autograph?"

Eddie shook his head and smiled. "That was the worst part."

"Huh?" Arnold said.

"This is kind of complicated," Eddie explained, "but I don't think that's really Helicopter Jones—not all of him, anyway. They just use tricks to make it look like he's all there."

"Huh?" Arnold said again.

Eddie sighed. "Think about it. The real Helicopter Jones doesn't care whether you wear his stupid shoes or not. The only thing he cares about is getting paid for putting his face in the commercial. So all you really see is the part of him that got paid for telling you how great the shoes are."

Arnold looked very disappointed.

"I know," Eddie said. "It's kind of a letdown. But nobody there tells the real truth. They don't even want to *know* the truth. They just give you a bunch of stories about how great everything is, even if they've only tried it for fifteen seconds. What a bunch of phonies!"

"So how come Will's so happy there?" Arnold asked.

"Because he doesn't know any better, I guess." Eddie shook his head.

"How did you know to take his shoes off?"

"What do you think? I'm not stupid. I figured out what was going on. But believe me, it wasn't easy. Every time I took off the shoes, somebody yelled at me to put them back on. But I was positive I'd never get back as long as I was wearing them."

"So why did you make all those faces and do all that silly stuff?"

"I had to do something. I didn't want anybody to think I was just like everybody else in the commercial. I figured maybe they'd kick me out. And I guess that's what they did. Hey, how did you figure out to make Will wear your shoes?"

Arnold made a face. "What do you think?" he echoed. "I'm not stupid."

"And boy, am I glad of that!" Eddie said. "Whew! I'm sure glad it's over and done with."

Arnold sighed. "Not exactly."

"What do you mean?" Eddie asked.

"Now instead of one broken TV set, I've got two. Not counting the one at the mall."

Eddie looked at the TV set behind him. "What's broken about this one?"

"Come on, Eddie," Arnold demanded. "Get serious!"

"I am serious," Eddie said. "What's broken about it?"

Arnold looked at the TV set again. Nothing seemed to be broken. The screen was actually in one piece. "But I saw it break!" Arnold insisted. "I heard the glass shatter."

"Looks fine now," Eddie said.

Arnold switched on the TV. "A local woman gives dozens of area salamanders a new home," announced a newscaster. "We'll have all the details right after this."

Arnold pressed the off button. "I saw it break. I heard it break. Now it's fine. I don't get it."

Eddie shrugged. "Me, neither. It's kind of like magic. But it's nothing to complain about."

"You said it!" Arnold exclaimed. "Hey, come on!" And he rushed out of the room.

In his stocking feet Eddie followed him downstairs. "What are you looking for?"

"The living room TV! It's not broken anymore!" Arnold cried. "It's here again, and it looks good as new!"

"Is that the one you broke last night when this whole thing started?" Eddie asked.

Arnold nodded and turned on the TV. "Chocolate lake stalls traffic. When *News Seven* continues," announced an anchorwoman.

A denture-adhesive commercial filled the screen. "Works fine now," Arnold said.

"Weird," Eddie declared. "Spooky. Must be more magic at work."

Arnold grabbed a piece of paper from the top of the TV set. He read it and handed it to Eddie. "Some magic!"

Eddie chuckled. "A bill from Aunt Edna's TV Repair Service. One hundred twenty-seven dollars and forty-three cents. Spooky, all right."

"About a year's worth of allowance is all." Arnold shuddered. "Maybe they won't make me pay back *every* penny of it." Shaking his head, he reached for the off switch.

"Wait!" Eddie cried.

Arnold stopped: It was the Helicopter Shoes commercial. Will was right at the front of the group, singing and dancing.

Helicopter
Helicopter
Helicopter Shoes.

Helicopter

Helicopter
Helicopter Shoes.

We're talking
Helicopter
Helicopter
Helicopter Shoes.

"He doesn't look any different," Arnold said. "I wonder what happened to those blisters of his."

"Ha!" said Eddie. "He'll just have to smile right through them. He'll have to keep pretending everything's perfectly wonderful, no matter what. That's the rule there."

Hey, Helicopter here
And I just want to say
My Helicopter Shoes
Are the shoes of today!

You can dance and jump around
In any old shoes.
But mine are the ones
That will cure your blues.

"You think maybe Will will stick out his tongue, the way you did?" Arnold asked.

Helicopter

Helicopter
Helicopter Shoes.

"Don't bet on it," Eddie replied. "If he acts
up, they'll kick him out, just the way they did
with me. And he knows it."

We're talking
Helicopter
Helicopter
Helicopter Shoes.

In a way, Arnold was almost beginning to
miss Will. "You think maybe he'll wave at us or
something?" he asked.

My shoes are the best
And that's the truth.
You gotta move with the 'Copter
Or else you're uncouth.

"Wave at us?" Eddie snorted. "No way! That
would mean he was kind of human, almost. That
would mean things weren't perfect there."

Without these shoes
I couldn't be great
They're the shoes
That let me levitate.

"Well, he got all upset and angry before," Arnold said. "That was kind of human. I bet he does something just to sort of thank us."

Hey, I made the shot
And so will you
As long as you're wearing
My Helicopter shoe.

"See that?" Eddie pointed. "Helicopter Jones didn't change one bit, and Will won't either. How much you want to bet?"

Helicopter
Helicopter
Helicopter Shoes.

"No money," Arnold replied. "Just a bet."
"It's a deal," said Eddie. "Will won't do anything different."
Arnold stared at the screen and rooted desperately for Will to do something kind of human.

We're talking
Helicopter
Helicopter
Helicopter Shoes . . .

"See?" said Eddie.

"It's not over yet!" Arnold replied. "Come on, Will!"

"Forget it!" Eddie laughed as Will danced to the front of the screen.

Helicopter
Helicopter
Helicopter Shoes.

Arnold kept hoping, but it was too late. A giant toilet bowl replaced Will's smiling face on the screen. Arnold sighed. It wasn't the first time a TV commercial had disappointed him.

"Told you!" said Eddie. "It's not new!"

Arnold smiled a little. "It's not improved."

"And neither is Will," Eddie added.

"It's the same dumb old commercial as ever!" Arnold agreed. "How I could have fallen for it in the first place, I'll never know."

"Look at it this way," Eddie said. "We had an adventure. And maybe Mrs. Nofziger will take Will's advice and get plastic surgery."

That night when his parents came home, Arnold told them he'd lost his Helicopter Shoes—though he didn't tell them exactly how. They yelled and hollered and lectured, but in the end they decided Arnold wouldn't have to pay for the shoes. He just wouldn't get new ones. That was fine with Arnold, though he didn't think it was a good idea to say so.

His parents also decided he wouldn't have to pay back all of the $127.43 it cost to fix the TV set. He would just have to give up his allowance for a month and his TV privileges for two weeks. That was not just fine with Arnold, though he didn't think it was a good idea to say so.

The hardest part came later. His parents made him phone Grandma and tell her how much he liked her birthday present—without actually mentioning what had happened to it.

The next day at the playground Arnold wore his plain, beat-up old sneakers. He didn't have bounce-gas soles. He didn't have zigzag shoelaces. He wasn't Helicopter Jones. But he still dribbled like a pro. He could still make any shot he wanted to. Five in a row! Six in a row! Seven! Eight—well, even people with very expensive shoes miss once in a while.

And even though Arnold's Helicopter Shoes had disappeared, Eddie's birthday present to him wasn't a total loss. The basketball-shoe cleaner and preservative turned out to work just great on Arnold's new basketball.

About the Author

Stephen Manes is an author, journalist, and screenwriter. He has published more than twenty-five books, including the *Hooples* series, *The Obnoxious Jerks,* (which is available in a Bantam Starfire hardcover edition), *The Boy Who Turned Into a TV Set*, *Chicken Trek*, and the award-winning *Be a Perfect Person in Just Three Days!* which is available in a Bantam Skylark edition.

Mr. Manes is a contributing editor and regular columnist for *PC Magazine*. He codeveloped Bantam's *StarFixer* software and wrote *The Complete MCI Mail Handbook*. With Ron Barrett he created *Encyclopedia Placematica*, the world's first book of place mats. He and his books have been the subject of several public television programs.

Wild and crazy adventures from
Stephen Manes!

☐ **BE A PERFECT PERSON IN
JUST THREE DAYS!**   15580-6 $3.25

Milo Crinkley tries to follow the loony instructions on being
perfect, found in a library book. But who ever heard of wearing
a stalk of broccoli around your neck for twenty-four hours? And
that's only the first day...

☐ **IT'S NEW! IT'S IMPROVED!
IT'S TERRIBLE!**   15682-9 $2.99

The TV commercials say the shoes that basketball star Ralph
"Helicopter" Jones wears are "New! IMPROVED! Amazing!
NEAT!" Arnold Schlemp just has to have them. At least until
the commercial steps out of his TV set and into his life!

☐ **CHICKEN TREK**   15716-7 $2.99

Oscar Noodleman spends his summer vacation entering the
"Chicken in the Bag" contest and eating 211 chicken meals at
restaurants across America! But Oscar's not the only one after
the $99,999.99 prize. Join the Chicken Trek!

Buy them at your local bookstore or use this page to order:

THE BEST OF SKYLARK

☐ **BIG RED**   by Jim Kjelgaard
0-553-15434-6 $2.99/$3.50 in Canada
Danny and an Irish setter named Red form a special
bond as they struggle for survival in the harsh wilderness
of the Wintapi.

☐ **THE INCREDIBLE JOURNEY**   by Sheila Burnford
0-553-15616-0 $3.99/not available in Canada
Three house pets, two dogs and a cat, face starvation,
exposure and wild forest animals to make their way
home to the family they love.

☐ **SEAL CHILD**   by Sylvia Peck
0-553-15868-6 $3.50/$3.95 in Canada
One summer Molly comes across a slain mother seal,
and meets a mysterious girl named Meara. Nothing can
prepare her for the strange truth...or for the dramatic
event that's about to change their lives—and their friend-
ship—forever.